For our parents, for being brave.

Copyright © 2002 by Elisabeth Jones and James Coplestone
All rights reserved

Published in 2002 in the United States by Ragged Bears
413 Sixth Avenue, Brooklyn, New York 11215
www.raggedbears.com

Simultaneously published in Great Britain by Ragged Bears
Milborne Wick, Sherborne, Dorset DT9 4PW

CIP Data is available

First American Edition
Printed in China
ISBN 1-929927-42-8
2 4 6 8 10 9 7 5 3 1

Moonlight & Shadow

Written by Elisabeth Jones
Illustrated by James Coplestone

RAGGED BEARS

Brooklyn, New York • Milborne Wick, Dorset

S

Alone in his new field,
Moonlight watched the world's
colors fade into night.

Big, soft snowflakes
began to fall around
the young horse.

The snow covered the field
until it gleamed
like crisp white paper
in the light of the moon.

Moon-shadows
fell across the land.

It was as though everything which stood tall was dreaming it could lie down and sleep.

Caught between the moonlight and the snow, these dreams could be seen.

Out of the corner of his eye,
Moonlight saw something move...

...it was a **BIG BLACK HORSE!**

Moonlight snorted and reared up in fear.
The big black horse reared up too,
bigger and blacker than ever.

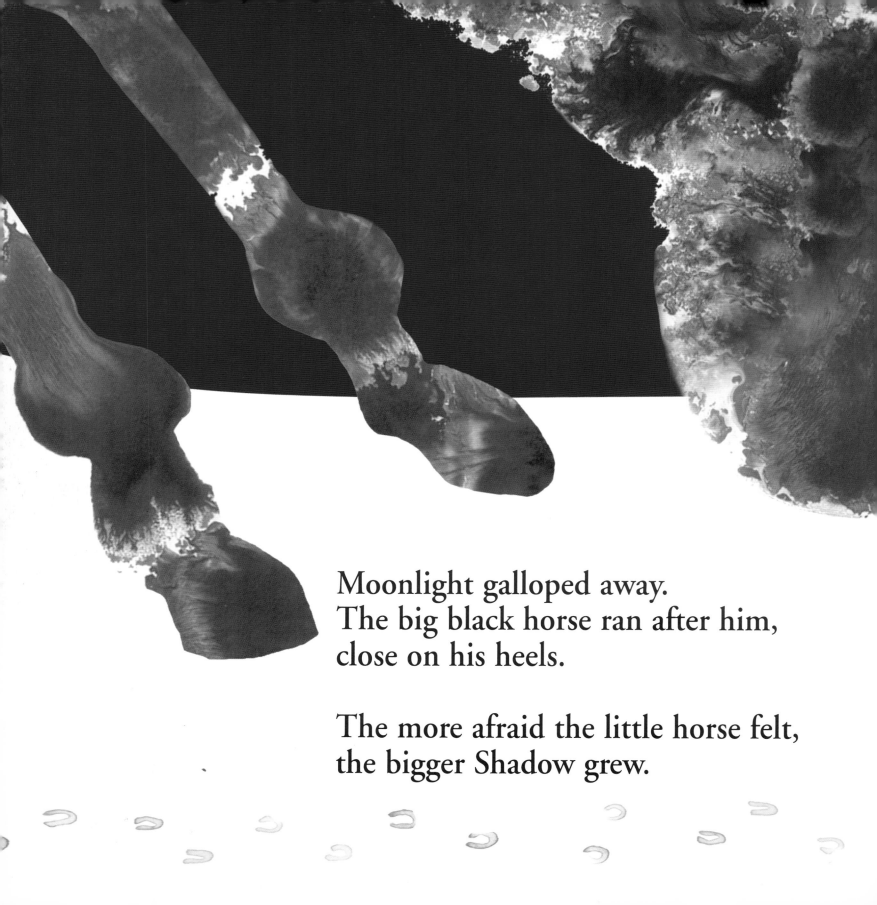

Moonlight galloped away.
The big black horse ran after him,
close on his heels.

The more afraid the little horse felt,
the bigger Shadow grew.

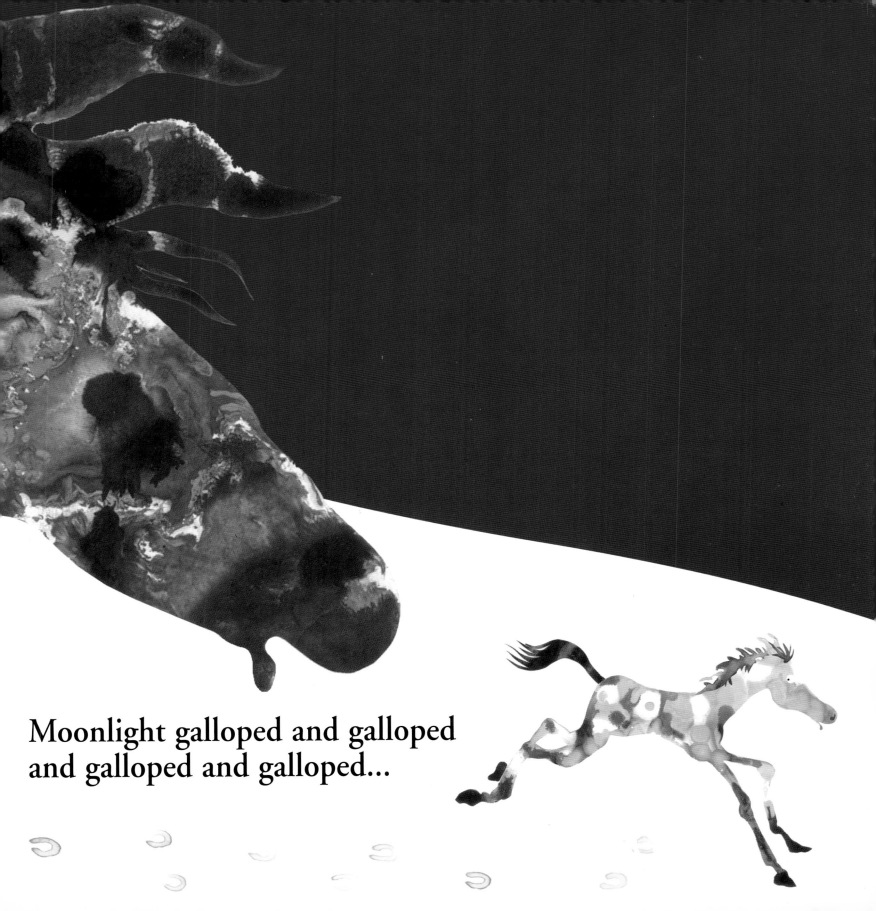

Moonlight galloped and galloped
and galloped and galloped...

to the very
dge of the field.

Moonlight was
apped by the fence.
here was nowhere
se for him to run.

Moonlight knew he must turn
to face the big, black horse.

Trembling with fear,
he slowly turned around.

There, touching his hooves,
were Shadow's hooves!

Moonlight put his muzzle towards
Shadow and sniffed.

Shadow smelled only of snow.
Moonlight's fears melted.

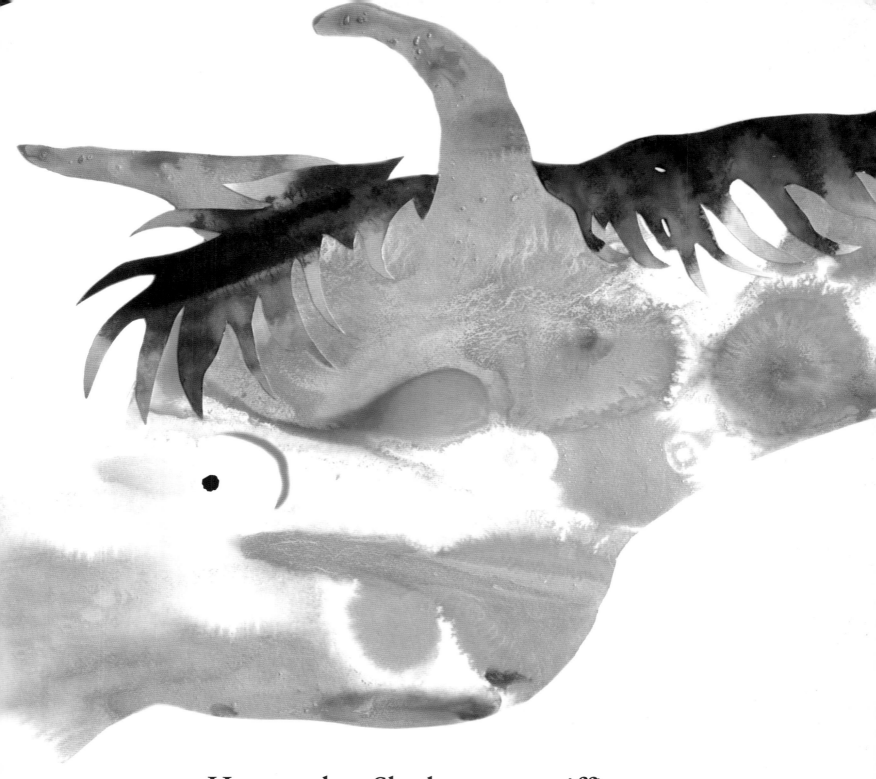

He saw that Shadow was sniffing too.
Perhaps Shadow wanted to be friends?

Moonlight nodded
his head at Shadow.
Shadow's head nodded back.

Shadow had been a **friend** all along!

Moonlight yawned an
ENORMOUS YAWN.
Shadow yawned too.

Moonlight lay down peacefully, knowing that Shadow would always be beside him.

Sleep drifted over them gently, like a cloud covering the moon.